Animal Fair

Animal Fair

adapted and illustrated by
Janet Stevens

Holiday House, New York

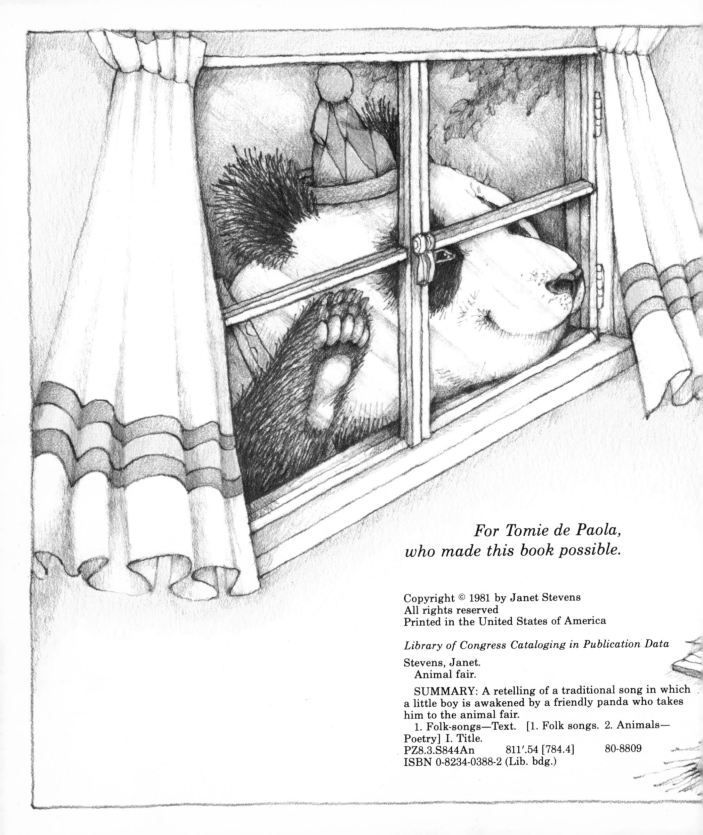

For Tomie de Paola,
who made this book possible.

Library of Congress Cataloging in Publication Data

Stevens, Janet.
    Animal fair.

    SUMMARY: A retelling of a traditional song in which
a little boy is awakened by a friendly panda who takes
him to the animal fair.

    1. Folk-songs—Text. [1. Folk songs. 2. Animals—
Poetry] I. Title.
PZ8.3.S844An   811'.54 [784.4]   80-8809
ISBN 0-8234-0388-2 (Lib. bdg.)

I went to the animal fair,

The birds . . .

And the beasts were there;

The big baboon
By the light of the moon
Was combing his auburn hair.

The monkey, he got drunk

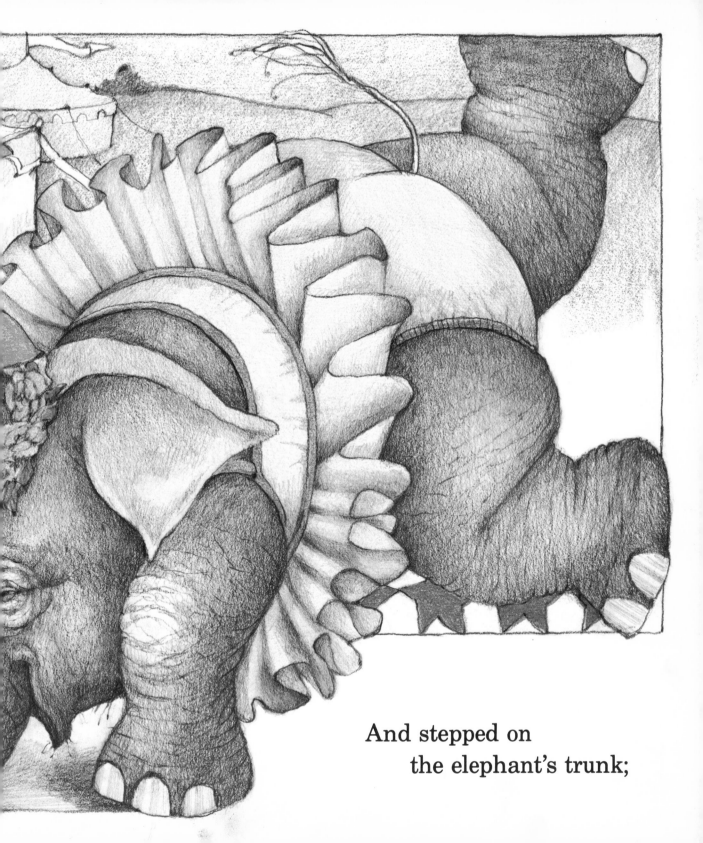

And stepped on
the elephant's trunk;

The elephant sneezed

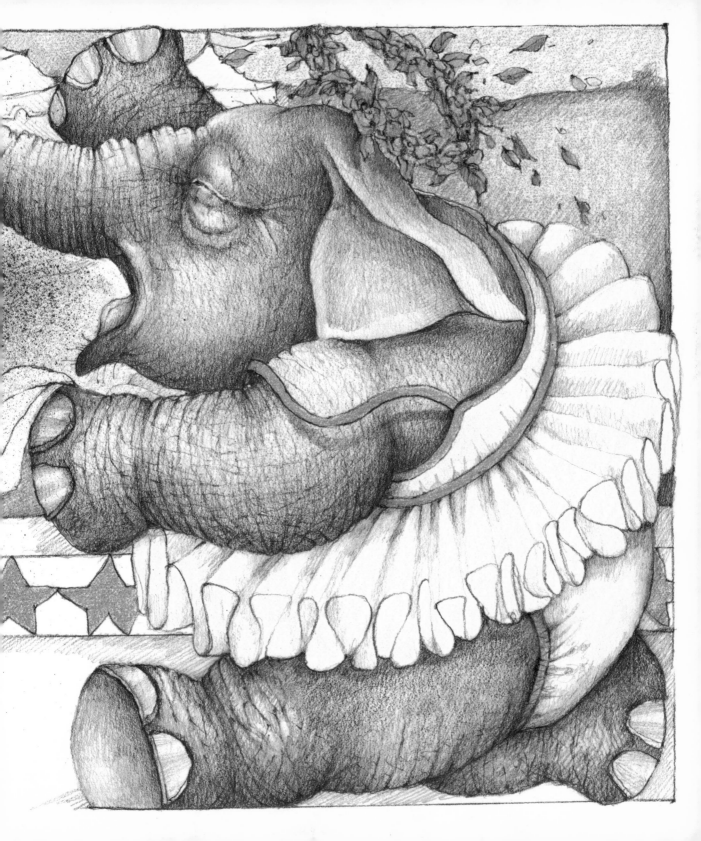

And fell on his knees

And that was the end of the monk,

The monk, the monk, the monk,

And that was the end of the monk!

Animal Fair

Arranged by Jamie Kibben